Jewish Americans

Amy Stone

Curriculum Consultant: Michael Koren,
Social Studies Teacher, Maple Dale School, Fox Point, Wisconsin

WORLD ALMANAC® LIBRARY

Please visit our web site at: www.garethstevens.com
For a free color catalog describing World Almanac® Library's
list of high-quality books and multimedia programs,
call 1-800-848-2928 (USA) or 1-800-387-3178 (Canada).
World Almanac® Library's fax: (414) 332-3567.

Library of Congress Cataloging-in-Publication Data

Stone, Amy, 1947-
    Jewish Americans / by Amy Stone.
       p. cm. — (World Almanac Library of American immigration)
    Includes bibliographical references and index.
    ISBN-10: 0-8368-7314-9 — ISBN-13: 978-0-8368-7314-6 (lib. bdg.)
    ISBN-10: 0-8368-7327-0 — ISBN-13: 978-0-8368-7327-6 (softcover)
    1. Jews—United States—History—Juvenile literature. 2. Judaism—United
States—Juvenile literature. 3. United States—Civilization—Jewish influences—
Juvenile literature. I. Title. II. Series.
    E184.35.S76   2007
    973'.04924—dc22   2006005324

First published in 2007 by
World Almanac® Library
A member of the WRC Media Family of Companies
330 West Olive Street, Suite 100
Milwaukee, WI 53212, USA

Copyright © 2007 by World Almanac® Library.

Produced by Discovery Books
Editors: Jacqueline Laks Gorman and Sabrina Crewe
Designer and page production: Sabine Beaupré
Photo researcher: Sabrina Crewe
Maps and diagrams: Stefan Chabluk
Consultant: Maddalena Marinari
World Almanac® Library editorial direction: Mark J. Sachner
World Almanac® Library editor: Barbara Kiely Miller
World Almanac® Library art direction: Tammy West
World Almanac® Library production: Jessica Morris

Picture credits: American Jewish Archives: 24; CORBIS: title page, 5, 17, 42; Getty
Images: 11, 36, 37, 39, 41, 43; Library of Congress: cover, 9, 13, 16, 18, 19, 20–21,
22, 23, 25, 26, 28 (both), 29, 30, 31, 33, 34, 35; National Park Service: 10; North
Wind Picture Archives: 14; Topfoto.co.uk: 27; United States Holocaust Memorial
Museum: 40.

Printed in the United States of America

1 2 3 4 5 6 7 8 9 10 09 08 07 06

Contents

Front cover: A group of newsboys in the early 1900s waits outside the publishing office of the *Jewish Daily Forward* at 1:00 A.M. Although education was important in Jewish American families, many children had to work to help their families survive.

Title page: Jewish Americans observe Shabbat, a day of rest and spiritual reflection that lasts from sunset on Friday to just after sunset on Saturday. The ritual lighting of candles is part of the Shabbat tradition.

Introduction

The United States has often been called "a nation of immigrants." With the exception of Native Americans—who have inhabited North America for thousands of years—all Americans can trace their roots to other parts of the world.

Immigration is not a thing of the past. More than seventy million people came to the United States between 1820 and 2005. One-fifth of that total— about fourteen million people—immigrated since the start of 1990. Overall, more people have immigrated permanently to the United States than to any other single nation.

Push and Pull

Historians write of the "push" and "pull" factors that lead people to emigrate. "Push" factors are the conditions in the homeland that convince people to leave. Many immigrants to the United States were—and still are—fleeing persecution or poverty. "Pull" factors are those that attract people to settle in another country. The dream of freedom or jobs or both continues to pull immigrants to the United States. People from many countries around the world view the United States as a place of opportunity.

Building a Nation

Immigrants to the United States have not always found what they expected. People worked long hours for little pay, often doing jobs that others did not want to do. Many groups also endured prejudice.

"Once in a while, I would ask my father about life in the old country. He would shrug and say, 'You shouldn't know from it.' He had come here, at age thirteen, from a small village in Poland and his family had been extremely poor. . . . He started clerking in a dry goods store. He worked there until he retired . . . never missing a day of work—not one single day. My father had found the better life he wanted and he clung to it—with a passion."

Gary Rachelefsky, a Jewish American doctor, remembering his father's immigration story

▲ A boy studies for his Bar Mitzvah at a synagogue in New Jersey in 2005 by reading the Torah, which is the Hebrew name for the first five books of the Bible. Jewish Americans share their ancient faith and sense of history with Jews around the world.

In spite of these challenges, immigrants and their children built the United States of America, from its farms, railroads, and computer industries to its beliefs and traditions. They have enriched American life with their culture and ideas. Although they honor their heritage, most immigrants and their descendants are proud to call themselves Americans first and foremost.

A Triumph of Survival

For thousands of years, Jews in many countries have faced prejudice and persecution—even death—primarily because of their religious beliefs. They were forced to leave their homelands and build new lives in new places. The first Jews settled in America in 1654. From that point onward, the number of Jewish immigrants to America grew, slightly at first and later by large numbers.

Nearly 250,000 German and other central European Jews came to the United States between 1820 and 1880. Between 1881 and 1924, during what is called the "Great Migration," about two million eastern European Jews came. More arrived after World War II and the Holocaust, during which six million European Jews were killed. Today, there are about 5.3 million Jews in the United States, making up almost 2 percent of the U.S. population.

When Jewish Americans today raise their glasses to make a toast, they often say "*l'chaim*," which in Hebrew means "to life." The phrase celebrates more than 350 years of Jewish life in the United States as well as the triumph of their survival as a people.

Life in
the Homeland

Jews came to the United States from a number of countries. Thousands of years ago, Jews lived in Palestine—most of which is now the nation of Israel in the Middle East. Their land was conquered by other nations, and the Jews were forced into exile. Some settled in other parts of the Middle East, others went to Africa, while many moved to Europe. Wherever Jews went, they took their religion and traditions with them. Many Jews faced prejudice and did not enjoy equal rights in their new homelands. Whatever their background and homeland, most Jews emigrated to the United States for the same reasons: to escape poverty and persecution and to make a better life.

The Jews of Spain

By the eighth century, the land that is now Spain was under Muslim rule, and Jews there were treated almost as equals. Many excelled as scientists, geographers, poets, and doctors. By the middle of the 1400s, however, Christians had taken control of Spain. Christians were not tolerant of other religions, and they were especially hostile to Jews because they believed that Jewish authorities were to blame for the death of Jesus Christ. This belief would be at the root of much Christian persecution of Jews for centuries to come. In the late 1400s, the king and queen of Spain began the Inquisition, a program to find and punish people who were not Christians, including Jews. If Jews refused to convert to Christianity, they were imprisoned, tortured, or killed. Some Jews pretended to convert but still secretly practiced their religion.

In 1492, Spain sent Christopher Columbus to the Americas; it also expelled all its Jews. Many fled to Portugal, where other Jews had practiced their religion openly for hundreds of years. Before long, however, the Inquisition spread to Portugal. To escape the

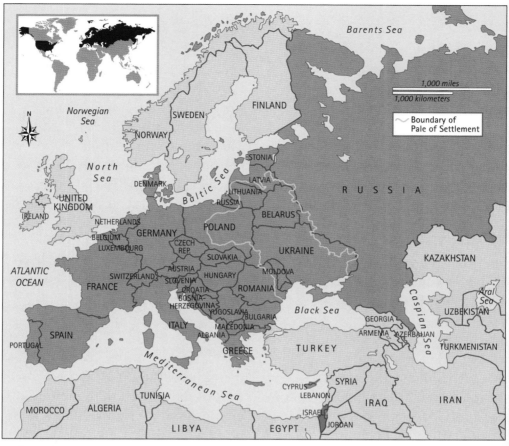

Jews live in nations all over the world, but most Jews came to the United States from the areas that are colored darker on this map. Today, the Jews have a homeland in Israel (highlighted in green), which was founded in 1948.

Inquisition, many Sephardic Jews then went to the Netherlands. Their descendants helped the Dutch set up colonies in South America. When Portugal took control of a Dutch colony in Recife, Brazil, in 1654, however, the Jews there were expelled. Twenty-three ended up in North America, in the city of New Amsterdam (later renamed New York), becoming the first Jews to settle in what would become the United States.

The Jews of Central Europe

While Sephardic Jews were living in Spain, Portugal, and Africa, other Jews lived in cities and states in central Europe that eventually became part of Germany. Jews faced religious persecution there, too. In 1095, the Roman Catholic Church began the Crusades, a plan to "free" the Holy Land in the Middle East from Muslim rule. The Crusaders saw all non-Christians, including Jews, as their enemies.

Ashkenazim and Sephardim

Jews are often divided into two groups: Ashkenazim and Sephardim. After being turned out of their Middle Eastern homeland about two thousand years ago, Jews who settled in central and eastern Europe (and eventually throughout western Europe) came to be called Ashkenazim, from the Hebrew word for "German." Jews who settled in Spain, Portugal, and other southern European nations—as well as the Middle East and North Africa—became known as Sephardim, from the Hebrew word for "Spaniard." Over hundreds of years, each group acquired customs that distinguished it from the other. While the Jews of central and eastern Europe developed the Yiddish language, Sephardic communities developed Ladino, a language that combines Hebrew, Spanish, Portuguese, and Arabic. Despite their cultural and linguistic differences, the Sephardim and Ashkenazim share many traditions and one critical feature—their historical and religious identity as Jews. Today, most Jews in the United States are Ashkenazic Jews.

Over the next few hundred years, as they traveled through Europe and once they reached the Middle East, the Crusaders killed thousands of Jews and Muslims. Other Christians shunned Jews because they would not adopt Christianity.

Jews also faced laws restricting their rights. They could not own land or do agricultural work. Many were forced to live separately from Christians in ghettos, crowded parts of cities that were set apart and often had walls around them. Over time, Jews in these communities began speaking Yiddish, a unique language that included elements of German, Slavic languages, and Hebrew, the Jewish language. Yiddish became the language of most Ashkenazim.

Reasons to Emigrate

While conditions improved somewhat, Jews in Germany still suffered from injustice. Before 1871, Germany was not a united country. It consisted of small states led by wealthy rulers. In most German states, Jews could not hold office or vote. Jews also could not own land, so many worked as merchants, tradesmen, and moneylenders.

The population of Germany grew during the 1700s, and jobs became scarce for all Germans. In addition, by the 1800s, the central European economy was changing from agricultural to industrial. Many non-Jewish farmers moved to the cities while others emigrated to the United States. These departures robbed Jews of their livelihood, since many had sold goods or lent money to non-Jewish farmers. When news of opportunities in the United States reached Germany, thousands of Jews decided to emigrate, too.

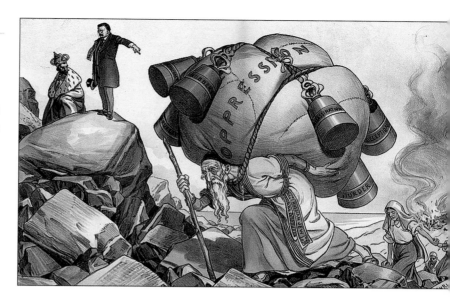

▶ A 1904 drawing published in a U.S. magazine shows how people in the United States viewed Russia's treatment of Jews. In the background (*left*), U.S. president Theodore Roosevelt demands that Czar Nicholas II stop his cruel oppression.

Another cause of emigration was a failed revolution against the German rulers. In 1848, Germans had revolted after their rulers refused to grant them such rights as trial by jury and the freedom to hold meetings. The revolution was short and unsuccessful. Many of the intellectuals who supported the revolution were Jews who had hoped it would result in more rights for Jews and other Germans. Some of them decided to emigrate to the United States.

The Jews of Eastern Europe

The homelands of eastern European Jews differed from those of central European Jews in significant ways. Beginning in the late 1700s, about 95 percent of eastern European Jews were forced by their Russian rulers to live in an area called the Pale of Settlement. The region comprised twenty-five Russian provinces between the Baltic Sea and the Black Sea. The Pale of Settlement, a small part of a larger Russian empire, included eastern Poland and most of present-day Lithuania, Belarus, Moldova, and Ukraine.

Life in the Pale of Settlement

Jews in the Pale could not vote, own land, or hold office. They paid higher taxes than non-Jews. Boys were forced to serve in the military for long periods of time. Some Jews in the Pale lived in remote, isolated villages called *shtetls*. Others lived in larger villages, towns, and cities. While a few urban families were wealthy, most were poor and lived in crowded conditions.

Most families living in the Pale in the 1800s struggled to survive. From dawn to dusk, men worked in clothing stores, grocery

◀ During the pogroms, the parents of these Russian children were massacred. The children were brought to the United States, where they were photographed on arrival in New York City in 1908.

"Our home was nothing special. . . . The floor was plain wooden boards, slats. I remember they were roughly made and there was earth in between. . . . My grandfather used to climb on top of the oven and sleep there because it was warm from the cooking. . . . I think he went up there because he was advanced in age and the house probably wasn't very warm."

Morris Hochstadt, recalling his home in the village of Lucenec, Slovakia, before he came to the United States as a young boy in the early 1900s

shops, or small factories. Skilled tradesmen, such as carpenters, often did not have enough work in their hometowns. To get more work, they had to travel throughout the countryside for weeks at a time. Women worked in the home and ran family shops. To increase the family income, they often took in extra work, such as rolling cigars.

Although Jews living in the Pale of Settlement were limited in the jobs they were allowed to do, their occupations would later help them find work. When eastern European Jews emigrated to the United States, much of their work was in retail, in small factories, and as skilled tradespeople.

Russian authorities let only a few Jewish children attend public schools. Young Jewish boys learned Hebrew and religion at a small school called a *cheder*. If the family could afford it, older boys then went to a *yeshiva* for advanced religious studies. At home, girls learned the basics of Jewish law, so they could keep a kosher home (one that followed religious dietary laws) when they married and had children. Russia's rulers let only a small number of Jews pursue higher education, which allowed these Jews to get better jobs.

The Pogroms

The anti-Semitism that had been brewing in Russia for years boiled over in 1881, after the assassination of the Russian ruler, Czar Alexander II. Christian peasants wrongly blamed

Jews for the czar's death. In the Pale of Settlement, mobs of peasants looted Jewish stores, burned Jewish homes, and murdered Jewish citizens. The government did nothing to stop them.

This massacre, called a pogrom, triggered hundreds more over the next forty years, occurring in three waves through 1920. One of the worst took place on April 6 and 7, 1903, when a pogrom in the city of Kishinev left about fifty Jews dead and some five hundred wounded, with seven hundred Jewish homes burned to the ground.

A Common Religious Bond

No matter which homeland they came from, Jews had one thing in common: their religion. Jews in Spain, Germany, or Russia—or other countries—might have different languages and customs. They shared the same religious history, however, as well as the same ancient language, Hebrew, and the same sacred writings (called the Torah). They celebrated the same Sabbath (called *Shabbos* or *Shabbat*, observed on Saturday) and the same holidays, reciting most of the same prayers. They all believed that Jews were God's "chosen people," which meant they carried with them special duties and responsibilities, including caring for one another and performing kind and charitable acts.

▶ Men wearing *talit*, or prayer shawls, cover their heads during services for the Jewish holiday of Sukkot at the Western Wall in Jerusalem, Israel. Traditionally, Sukkot was marked by a pilgrimage to Jerusalem at the end of the harvest season.

"We looked across the village and we saw them [the Russian soldiers] kill our grandparents—they fell over dead. Then they came after us. . . . But we escaped because we had money. They let us go. We were lucky. . . . We walked through. Where we walked there were woods, and there were sharp bushes and the bushes made our legs bleed. We went to Romania first. I don't remember how we got to Romania, I only remember walking."

Hannah Toperoff, who spent her early childhood in the town of Proskurov in Ukraine, remembering the terrifying incident that triggered her family's departure; the family eventually emigrated to the United States

CHAPTER 2

Emigration

"Before sunset the news was all over Polotzk that Hannah Hayye had received a steamer ticket for America. Then they began to come. Friends and foes, distant relatives and new acquaintances, young and old, wise and foolish . . . poured into our street . . . 'til the hour of our departure. . . . And my mother gave audience. Her faded kerchief halfway off her head, her black ringlets straying, her apron often at her eyes, she received her guests in a rainbow of smiles and tears. She was the heroine of Polotzk, and she conducted herself appropriately. . . . They wanted to handle the ticket, and mother must read them what is written on it."

Mary Antin, recalling the excitement caused in her home town of Polotzk, Russia, when her family received tickets to travel to the United States in the late 1800s

Depending on when they came to the United States, Jews experienced different journeys. None of them, however, was easy. The twenty-three Sephardic Jews who fled Recife, Brazil, in 1654 had a difficult trip. They spent weeks on a cramped wooden sailing ship, the *Sainte Catherine,* experiencing seasickness, piracy, and near starvation. The Jews who left Europe in later years to escape persecution and help colonize America also endured difficult journeys. Their sailing ships took six to ten weeks to cross the Atlantic, subjecting passengers to crowded quarters, unsanitary conditions, little (or spoiled) food, and rough seas.

Steamships had been invented when German Jews began to emigrate in the 1820s. The trip then took only three weeks. The shorter trip, combined with the poverty and persecution at home, probably explains why so many emigrants in the 1800s made the decision to leave their homelands for the United States.

The Promise of a Better Life
Books and pamphlets also influenced people's decisions to leave for the United States. A Yiddish translation

of the story of the European discovery of America sold thousands of copies in the 1840s. Penny booklets and novels told the legend of an America where streets were paved with gold, where everyone could make a fortune. Steamship ticket agents not only advertised the journey but often exaggerated the wonders of what was called the "Golden Land."

It is estimated that one out of three eastern European Jews emigrated to the United States between 1881 and 1920. Why did the rest decide to stay? Some were strict Orthodox Jews who believed it would be too difficult to maintain their traditions in a country that might not accept or support them. Others held on to hopes about the future of Jews in eastern Europe. They thought that as Russians became more educated, the restrictions against Jews would be lifted. Anti-Semitism, they hoped, would eventually disappear.

Still others lacked the means to make the expensive journey. Sometimes, families had to sell most of their possessions to buy steamship tickets. Many eastern European Jews, having never left their villages, found it difficult to

▲ The dream of the Golden Land was expressed in this 1917 poster. The U.S. government used the image of Jews arriving in America to remind people to be careful with resources during World War I. The Yiddish words read, "You came here seeking freedom, now you must help preserve it—Wheat is needed for the Allies—Waste nothing."

"My ancestors had lived there for centuries. . . . Now I was leaving it, the only home I had ever known. . . . Though my mother, brother, and sisters were with me, I felt the desolation of the uprooted. . . . I had loved the old home . . . and leaving it was like tearing something out of my very soul."

Maurice Hindus, who came to the United States from Russia in 1891 at the age of fourteen

Emigrants struggle to board a ship bound for the United States from Hamburg, Germany. Hamburg was one of the main points of departure for European Jews going to the United States.

" . . . We get on the train, and my grandfather was supposed to get on the train with us, and soldiers get on board . . . and start throwing off people because they needed the room. He was thrown off the train. My mother and we three were allowed to get on. And they never had a proper goodbye because they were torn from each other's arms. . . . My mother cried all her life, for the rest of her life, at the farewell she did not have with her father."

Jennie Grossman, remembering her late 1880s train journey across Poland to reach a port city

leave their homes for emotional reasons, too.

Unlike most other people who left for the United States in the same period, the eastern European Jews emigrated with the intention of settling permanently in the United States. Other Europeans, as well as Asians, often emigrated to earn money in the United States and then planned to return home.

The eastern Europeans who made the journey started writing home, encouraging relatives to follow. They told of a country where all children, Jews and non-Jews alike, could go to school. With surprise, they reported that skilled tradesmen—who had been looked down upon in eastern Europe for working with their hands—were admired in the United States. Some letters held steamship tickets, which caused great excitement not only for the recipients but for entire towns.

Facing Dangers and Discomfort

Laws against Jewish travel outside the Pale of Settlement made it dangerous to leave. Eastern European Jews often traveled at night to reach such port cities as Vienna, Austria; Liverpool, England; and Hamburg, Germany. Some traveled by train, while others hitched rides in farmers' carts. All emigrants feared that Russian officials would find and arrest them. To cross the Pale of Settlement borders, these emigrants either sneaked across unguarded spots or bribed the guards.

Once they reached the port cities, passage was not guaranteed. Port officials inspected prospective emigrants for evidence of such diseases as smallpox or typhus. If they found such evidence, the officers turned these hopeful travelers away.

In the later 1800s and early 1900s, the steamship trip across the Atlantic took only about six days. It nevertheless exposed emigrants to many discomforts. The traveling compartment within the steerage section of the ship (below the lowest deck) held about three hundred tightly packed men, women, and children. They slept or rested on two- or three-tiered bunks that were about 6 feet (1.8 meters) long and 2 feet (0.6 m) wide. Only about 2.5 feet (0.8 m) separated the bunks. Since there was no storage space on the ship, families had to keep their few belongings next to them on the bunks. This left little room for stretching out or sleeping. For fresh air, passengers climbed to the deck above, where it was also very crowded. Sophia Kreitzberg, who came to the United States from Russia in 1908, remembered, "The atmosphere was so thick and dense with smoke and bodily odors that your head itched, and when you scratched your head . . . you got lice on your hands."

"My grandmother endured terrible grief when she traveled by steamship to the United States in 1916, but not due to the sadness of leaving her homeland. When she lost track of her three-year-old son— my father—on the crowded deck, she believed he had fallen overboard. For nearly three days, she couldn't find him. Unable to sleep or eat, she cried and cried. By the fifth day, however, she found her son—a bit frightened but otherwise fine; another Jewish mother had taken good care of him."

Nancy Bornstein, a Jewish American, remembering a family immigration story

Most ships provided only one small tin can of water for each passenger once a day. There was also nonkosher meat and soup, which many travelers refused. Instead, they existed on supplies of dried fruit, hardened bread, or cheese they had brought with them.

Entering America

During the Great Migration of 1881 to 1924, about 70 percent of Jewish immigrants entered the United States through New York City. At first, they came through a receiving station there called Castle Garden. After 1892, they came through a station on Ellis Island in New York Harbor. Immigrants weary from their transatlantic journey found little relief at Ellis Island. The station was a busy place; in 1907, immigration officials there handled more than one million immigrants.

Upon arrival, doctors examined the immigrants to make sure they did not have any diseases. If people were found to be unhealthy, they would be refused entry and sent back to Europe. Then inspectors interviewed each immigrant, asking if he or she was joining relatives in the United States and had paid for his or her own passage. After 1907, immigrants were required to prove that they could read and write. The whole process was often tense and upsetting. Emma Goldman, who later became a famous political activist, described her arrival in New York from Russia in 1886:

▼ Immigrants wait on Ellis Island for a boat that will transfer them to New York City, where they will begin new lives as Americans.

Emma Lazarus and the Statue of Liberty

Beginning in 1886, when immigrants reached New York Harbor, many drew comfort from the sight of the magnificent Statue of Liberty. The statue became a symbol of shelter and freedom from oppression for people who were denied liberty and opportunity in their homelands. The base of the statue is inscribed with the poem "The New Colossus," written by Jewish American poet Emma Lazarus (1849–1887). Lazarus had not received a Jewish education while growing up, but she became interested in her religion after learning of the pogroms in Europe. She began working with Jewish immigrants and writing about Jewish causes. The last lines of the poem on the Statue of Liberty read:

> "Give me your tired, your poor,
> Your huddled masses yearning to breathe free,
> The wretched refuse of your teeming shore,
> Send these, the homeless, tempest-tossed to me,
> I lift my lamp beside the golden door!"

"We were surrounded by . . . angry men, hysterical women, screaming children. Guards roughly pushed us, . . . shouted orders to get ready. . . . Nowhere could one see a sympathetic official face; there was no provision for comfort of the new arrivals."

Yet they had arrived. The streets of America may not have been paved with gold, but they offered opportunities and freedoms not available elsewhere.

▶ Jews continued to emigrate to the United States after the Great Migration, most notably after the Nazi persecution of Jews in Europe during World War II. This Czech family with twelve children survived the war and arrived in 1949.

CHAPTER 3

Arriving in the United States

The story of Jewish Americans begins with the handful of Sephardic refugees from Recife, Brazil. They landed in New Amsterdam, now New York City, in 1654.

The Earliest Arrivals

Peter Stuyvesant, the anti-Semitic governor of the colony of New Amsterdam, did not want the Jews to stay. He wrote to his employers, the Dutch West India Company, that he believed the Jews threatened to "infect and trouble this new colony." The Jews launched a fight. They wrote to the company as well, pointing out that they and their ancestors had been Dutch citizens for centuries. They asserted their right to ". . . live freely wherever the Dutch flag flew." Partly because some of the company owners were Jews, the company ruled that the Jews could stay—as long as they took care of their own poor and expected no charity from Christians.

▼ Peddlers traveled across the United States in the 1800s to small towns and farming regions. In this 1868 drawing, a peddler carrying all kinds of household goods is showing a piece of fabric to his customers.

▲ Most Jewish immigrants, such as these newcomers from Russia in New York City, arrived in the United States with little money and only the possessions they could carry.

More Jews arrived, in small numbers at first. They learned English and found their places in American society. The fact that the Jewish population was so small, however, made it hard to maintain their religion. Rebecca Samuel, who lived in Petersburg, Virginia, in the late 1700s, wrote to her parents in Germany, "Jewishness is pushed aside here. There are here [in Petersburg] ten or twelve Jews, and they are not worthy of being called Jews. . . . You can believe me that I crave to see a synagogue to which I can go."

Favorable Opportunities

When central European Jews arrived between 1820 and 1880, the United States was in the midst of economic change. The country's population was growing. The demand for goods had grown as well, and immigrant Jews helped to meet it.

After landing in port cities, many central European Jewish immigrants—mostly ambitious men in their late teens or twenties—began their careers as peddlers. Walking with packs on their backs or driving horse-drawn wagons, they fanned out across the United States. Along the back roads of such states as Ohio, Michigan, Illinois, Wisconsin, Minnesota, Missouri, and Montana, these immigrants sold second-hand clothing, cheap jewelry, dishes, buttons, needles, and thread. (The goods were usually bought on credit.) Their customers welcomed them, bought their goods, and helped them learn English. The immigrants then invested their profits into farming tools and more expensive goods. They sold these items and made even more money. Over time, many of these peddlers used their savings to start banks, factories, and retail stores. Many major department stores—such as Macy's, Altman's, Rich's, and Bloomingdale's—were begun by German Jewish immigrants.

Levi's Jeans

Eighteen-year-old Levi Strauss emigrated from Bavaria in Germany to New York in 1847. His older brothers had already come to the United States and started a dry goods business. When the Gold Rush began, Strauss headed to San Francisco, California, to set up a new business. He became known as a fair and honest man, a city leader, and a generous donor to Jewish charities. Strauss also made a fortune manufacturing a new kind of heavy denim pants with strong seams. The jeans were Levi's, and today Levi Strauss & Co. is one of the world's largest clothing manufacturers.

▲ Hester Street, photographed here in 1902, was the center of Jewish life on New York City's Lower East Side. Lined with Jewish businesses and street vendors with pushcarts, it bustled with activity.

In 1825, the newly built Erie Canal linked New York City with the Great Lakes and the Midwest. In the years that followed, railroads made western states accessible, and people from the East Coast made their way west. They set up homesteads along the way. Jewish immigrants joined them. The discovery of gold in California in 1848 sparked a huge westward migration, opening up opportunities for Jews who worked mainly as merchants and storekeepers.

The path to such success, however, was not always smooth. Some Jewish immigrants who reached U.S. shores between 1820 and 1880 became very poor. Members of the wealthier German Jewish families banded together to help meet their needs, establishing agencies to help them.

The Lower East Side

Between 1881 and 1924, some two million eastern European Jews came to the United States. Entire families often came together. At times, complete shtetls came, carrying their sacred Torah scrolls.

Some eastern European Jews settled in such cities as Boston, Massachusetts; Philadelphia, Pennsylvania; Baltimore, Maryland; Cleveland, Ohio; and Chicago, Illinois. Most, however, made their

homes in the densely packed square mile
of New York City known as the Lower
East Side. The neighborhood was similar
in some ways to the homelands they had
left. People spoke Yiddish, and there were
synagogues and kosher butchers.

The majority of new immigrants
moved into tenement buildings, which
were usually about six stories tall, with
four small, four-room apartments on each
floor. The buildings were crowded and
airless and had no bathtubs or private
bathrooms. Instead, all the residents of each floor shared one
bathroom. Each apartment was often home to grandparents, aunts,
uncles, cousins, and friends as well as parents and children.

Competing for Jobs

Newly arrived immigrants had to find jobs. While U.S. cities of the
late 1800s and early 1900s had many retail, banking, and industrial
opportunities, they also teemed with people. Facing fierce competition, a number of eastern European immigrants took jobs that no
one else wanted. Some became peddlers, selling household goods
from pushcarts. Others found work as retail clerks, street cleaners,
or factory workers, especially in the garment industry. Tradespeople
worked as blacksmiths, electricians, mechanics, and bookbinders.
Jews with formal education entered such highly regarded professions
as medicine or law. Educated women, who were prevented from
entering such professions, settled for work in offices or as teachers.

CHAPTER 4

The Years 1654 to 1930

Jews came to the United States in small numbers from colonial times to 1880. By that year, there were about 250,000 Jews in the United States. Millions more came during the Great Migration, which lasted from 1881 to 1924. Their achievements, and sometimes their struggles, contributed to an ever-growing Jewish American culture and community.

The Early Years

After the Jews from Recife, Brazil, were given permission to stay in New Amsterdam in 1654, small numbers of other Jews followed. They arrived in the American colonies from England, France, the Netherlands, Germany, Poland, and European colonies. Some also came from Spain and Portugal, where they had lived as Conversos, or "Crypto-Jews"—Jews who converted to Christianity in order to save their lives—after the Inquisition of the late 1400s.

▼ The United States' oldest synagogue, the Touro Synagogue in Newport, Rhode Island, was used during the Civil War to shelter runaway slaves. It was designated as a National Historic Site in 1946.

During the colonial period, Jews settled along the East Coast and in several southern colonies. They established communities in Savannah, Georgia; Charleston, South Carolina; Philadelphia, Pennsylvania; and Newport, Rhode Island. The Sephardic community in Newport established the Jeshuat Israel congregation. They built the Touro Synagogue, which was consecrated (declared sacred for religious use) in 1763. Still standing today, it is the oldest synagogue in the United States.

▲ Rebecca Gratz was one of several Jewish women who helped poor immigrants.

Jews in the colonies faced restrictions. In some colonies, they could not vote, hold public office, or own property. They did enjoy religious freedom, however, and a better chance to earn a good living than they would have had in Europe.

During the American Revolution, one hundred Jews fought against the British. Haym Salomon, who had come to New York City from Poland, played an important role in helping finance the Continental Army. By 1800, about twenty-five hundred Jews lived in the United States. Charleston, with about five hundred Jews, had the largest community.

The First Large Wave

The first large wave of Jewish migration to the United States began during the 1820s. It was made up mostly of Jews from Germany and central Europe who were escaping poverty and unemployment as well as religious prejudice. While many Jews stayed on the East Coast, others headed west across the expanding United States. Jewish American immigrants found jobs manufacturing and selling goods, especially clothing. Some were modest peddlers and shopkeepers; others found wealth as bankers or became owners of large department stores.

In their new communities, Jews established synagogues and Jewish schools and charitable organizations. In Philadelphia in 1819, Rebecca Gratz founded the Female Hebrew Benevolent Society—the first Jewish women's group in the United States—to help the poor. In 1838, she founded the Hebrew Sunday School

◀ Michael Allen was the first known Jewish chaplain in the United States Army. He served as chaplain to the Cameron Dragoons during the Civil War and later became director of Hebrew studies at a Hebrew school in New York City.

Society. Many of the Jewish organizations that began during this time were social and political, not religious. One of these groups was B'nai B'rith (which means "Children of the Covenant"). It was formed by twelve young German immigrants in New York City in 1843 to provide services to the Jewish people and bring them together.

Jews were not just concerned with Jewish interests. They also became involved in social and political activities in their communities. Like all Americans, they were swept into the Civil War, which divided the nation in the 1860s. An estimated eight thousand to ten thousand Jewish Americans fought in the Civil War (most for the North, since most Jews lived in northern states). Perhaps the best known Jew during these years was Judah Benjamin, who was born in the Caribbean and grew up in South Carolina. Benjamin supported the South during the Civil War and was a member of the cabinet of Confederate president Jefferson Davis.

Religious Changes

Synagogues and religious life underwent many changes over the years. Ashkenazic Jews had become unhappy with the services of the mostly Sephardic congregations. They formed new Ashkenazic synagogues in many cities in the mid-1800s. At the same time, other Jews stopped participating in synagogue life altogether and were becoming less religious. They did not keep kosher or educate their children about Judaism. The rate of intermarriage (Jews marrying non-Jews) was rising. To combat these trends, some Jewish Americans became part of what was called the Reform movement. They wanted to change elements of Judaism so that it was better adapted to modern life in the United States. Services were shortened. Prayers were said in English as well as in Hebrew. The ban on seating men and women together was lifted. Choirs and organ music were incorporated into services for the first time.

▶ The grandest Reform synagogue in New York City was Temple Emanu-El (meaning "God is with Us"), shown here on its opening day in 1868. The Emanu-El congregation, founded in 1845 before the synagogue was built, was the first Reform congregation in the city.

The most important leader of the Reform movement was Rabbi Isaac Mayer Wise, who came to the United States from Bohemia in 1846. He settled in Cincinnati, Ohio, where he founded the Union of American Hebrew Congregations, a group of Reform synagogues, in 1873. He began Hebrew Union College, a school for Reform rabbis, two years later. By 1880, more than 90 percent of U.S. synagogues were Reform.

Some Jews thought that the Reform movement went too far in abandoning traditional Judaism. Since they felt that Orthodox Judaism was too strict, however, they started a third branch that fell between the two, called the Conservative movement. The three branches still exist today.

The Great Migration

In 1880, there were approximately 250,000 Jews in the United States, mostly from central Europe. Their numbers increased dramatically from 1881 to 1924, when some two million Jews entered the United States, mostly from eastern Europe. This Great Migration further shaped the story of Jewish Americans.

The new immigrants were often poor and less educated than the central European Jews who had come earlier. The new arrivals often spoke only Yiddish and came with few belongings. With their old-fashioned clothes, customs, and behavior, they were considered an embarrassment by the "established" Jews. The Jewish Americans of longer standing also feared that the new arrivals would cause an increase in anti-Semitism.

The established Jews, however, also felt a responsibility for the new arrivals. They created educational programs and organizations to help the new arrivals and teach them how to be Americans. In 1893, Hannah Solomon, the daughter of German immigrants, started the National Council of Jewish Women in Chicago, Illinois, to help newly arrived Jewish immigrants. One important service provided was a night school, where the immigrants learned language and vocational skills. Settlement houses—such as Lillian Wald's Henry Street Settlement in New York City and Minnie Low's Maxwell Street Settlement House in Chicago—helped immigrants with matters of health and employment. Eastern European Jews also set up their own groups to offer services.

School and Family Matters

In their desire to have their families fit in and get ahead, parents made sure their children attended the public schools. (Poor children, however—especially girls—had to leave school at about the sixth to eighth grade to go to work.) "Never was there such an awakening in people of the desire for learning," recalled Marie Jastrow, who came to New York from Serbia. "The concern of parents for the education of the children was the most important element in their lives." As children learned about the United States and American ways, however, tensions often arose within families. The children saw their parents as old-fashioned and were ashamed of them. The parents, on the other hand, simply did not understand their children.

▾ Girls learn knitting in a class at the Henry Street Settlement in New York City in 1910.

▲ The "old fashioned" appearance and behavior of many Jewish immigrants in the early 1900s set them apart from other Jewish Americans. Newly arrived immigrants, like those shown here, relied on Jewish groups to learn how to fit into U.S. society.

To get advice on these bewildering matters—and other troubling issues—immigrants wrote to the "Bintel Brief." This feature was the advice column of the leading Yiddish newspaper, the *Jewish Daily Forward*. Abraham Cahan began the newspaper in 1897, and it became known as "the voice of the Jewish immigrant." The "Bintel Brief" was soon the paper's most popular feature.

New Ideas

Many of the eastern European Jews who came during the latter half of the Great Migration believed in socialism. They believed that workers should own and control the "instruments of production," such as factories, mills, and railroads. Production, they argued, should satisfy human needs rather than the owners' desires for profits. These socialist ideas influenced the thinking of a number of Jews who later formed and led labor unions.

Working Conditions

In the workplace, meanwhile, new industrial processes were introduced in the late 1800s and early 1900s. The new processes created jobs for many Americans, including eastern European

"What is the point of the crazy game [of baseball]? It makes sense to teach a child to play dominoes or chess. But baseball? The children can get crippled . . ."

A bewildered father, writing for advice to the Jewish Daily Forward

"Watch yourself. The last kid working that punch machine lost all his fingers on one hand."

William Zorach, who landed his first U.S. factory job at age twelve, remembering advice he received from another youngster

▲ A Jewish American family works making garters in a tenement home in about 1912. Many Jewish American families endured terrible poverty in spite of their hard work.

Jewish immigrants. Garment (clothing) factories—primarily in New York, but also in other large cities—employed more eastern European immigrants than any other industry.

Although the factories employed mostly adults, they also employed children. Some of the poorest and largest immigrant families had no choice but to depend on their children's earnings to keep the families alive. Families set up shops in their apartments, with father, mother, and children all working together. Even when child labor was banned in 1938, children still went to work.

Factory workers suffered from unsafe and harsh working conditions. The factories were dark and dirty. Broken or poorly designed machines caused injuries. Wages were low even though many workers put in fourteen- to sixteen-hour days.

The Labor Movement

To fight against these conditions, workers organized, forming labor unions. Organizing efforts were often led by young, educated Jewish intellectuals as well as less educated immigrants who had struggled as poorly paid workers in their homelands.

▶ Samuel Gompers speaks to the U.S. government's Commission on Industrial Relations in 1915 as part of his lifelong campaign to gain rights for working people.

Samuel Gompers and David Dubinsky were two Jews who played key roles in the labor movement. Gompers, who came to the United States from England in 1863, rolled cigars in the family tenement apartment until going to work at a New York City cigar factory. He joined the cigar makers' union in 1864 and later became its president. In 1886, he became president of the American Federation of Labor, a union that exercised tremendous power. It won such important workers' rights as a shorter work week and higher wages.

After coming to the United States in 1911, Dubinsky (who was a socialist, a person believing in socialism) became a cloak cutter

The Triangle Shirtwaist Factory Fire

In 1911, the Triangle Shirtwaist Company factory occupied the top three floors of a ten-story building in New York City. It employed mostly young Jewish and Italian American women. An hour before quitting time on March 25, a fire broke out. Within seconds, flames spread to piles of fabric and cleaning fluids, producing a blaze that soon engulfed the entire factory. Some of the women pulled a fire hose from its case, only to discover that it had rotted. Others ran to a rear exit door but could not open it because it was locked. Many jumped to their deaths rather than be burned alive. The fire claimed 146 lives. The tragedy increased support for the goals of the labor unions. With public backing, the unions eventually succeeded in forcing factory owners to make workplaces safer.

▲ Police officers line up coffins holding the bodies of young women killed in the 1911 Triangle Shirtwaist factory fire.

Rose Schneiderman (1882–1972): Lifelong Labor Organizer

After Samuel Schneiderman died in 1892, his family—who had emigrated from Poland to New York's Lower East Side—could barely pay rent or buy groceries. To help out, thirteen-year-old Rose Schneiderman went to work as a salesclerk. She took a job in the garment industry a few years later. The poor working conditions made Schneiderman angry. Fueled by a sense of injustice and a growing belief in socialism, she organized the Jewish Socialist United Cloth Hat and Cap Makers' Union in 1903. In 1907, Schneiderman joined the Women's Trade Union League, became vice president, and showed great talent as a union organizer. She later worked with the ILGWU and was an adviser on labor issues to President Franklin D. Roosevelt.

and joined the International Ladies' Garment Workers Union (ILGWU). He was elected president of the union in 1932 and led it for thirty-four years. Dubinsky is credited with turning unions into strong forces that greatly improved the rights of workers.

Facing Anti-Semitism

The United States offered Jewish immigrants freedom from restrictions, safety from violence, and economic opportunity. It also, however, exposed them to prejudices they had hoped to leave behind. Anti-Semitism existed in the United States, and Jewish Americans had to face it.

As their numbers grew, Jews faced many forms of prejudice. Many Christians still blamed Jews as a whole for the death of Jesus Christ. In addition to this, some Jews were in businesses—such as lending money—that led prejudiced Christians to say that Jews were greedy and untrustworthy. Many non-Jews thought Jews looked and sounded "different," too. At its worst, this kind of prejudice allowed white Christians to view Jews as somehow less than human—the same attitude that had permitted the enslavement of African Americans to exist for hundreds of years.

Many businesses simply refused to hire Jews or to serve them. Well into the early 1900s, it was not unusual to see signs in restaurants and resorts that read: "No dogs or Jews."

Anti-Semitism was more widespread in rural areas, where the

Ku Klux Klan—formed after the Civil War to oppose the rights of blacks—began to take action against Jews as well. In the 1900s, however, anti-Semitism became an increasingly accepted fact of life across the nation. In the 1920s, automaker Henry Ford contributed to the climate of anti-Semitism with regular attacks on Jews in a weekly newspaper he owned. A number of leading universities, including Harvard in Cambridge, Massachusetts, adopted a different but still damaging kind of discrimination. Instead of banning Jews outright, they limited the number of Jews who could attend.

The End of the Great Migration

In 1921, Congress passed a law that limited the total number of immigrants who could enter the United States each year. It also set quotas, restricting the number who could come from any particular country, based on the proportion of people from each country who were living in the United States in 1920. In 1924, Congress passed another law that cut the numbers and proportions back still further. The 1924 law—called the National Origins Act—severely limited immigration from eastern Europe and Italy. An estimated fifty thousand Jews entered the United States in 1924. Only ten thousand came the next year, and the numbers continued to decline. The Great Migration was over.

▶ Americans expressed their prejudice against Jews in many ways. U.S. magazines published anti-Semitic cartoons, including this one from the late 1800s of a ship carrying Jewish immigrants to the United States. (Note the stereotypical "Jewish" features on the passengers, the fish, and even the boat.)

CHAPTER **5**

The 1930s and Beyond

By the 1930s, for the first time in history, more Jewish Americans had been born within the United States than outside the country. Most U.S.-born Jews felt at home in the United States. Unlike many of their immigrant parents and grandparents, the majority found it fairly easy to make a good living. This was especially true for those who received a good education and those who benefited from the economic boom that followed World War I. Many U.S.-born Jewish Americans found jobs as clerks, shopkeepers, and salesmen. Those who graduated from college often became teachers or managers. Still others—those who graduated from professional schools—became dentists, doctors, pharmacists, and lawyers.

The Entertainment Industry

Yiddish theater had been an important part of the Jewish American community since the 1890s, and as the years passed, Jewish Americans figured prominently in the entertainment industry. Well into the 1940s, any list of well-known comedians, singers, songwriters, playwrights, and composers seemed to consist almost entirely of Jews. Most of these entertainers had emigrated from eastern Europe or were the children of eastern European parents.

Composer Irving Berlin, who was born in Russia and came to the United States as a child, wrote many beloved songs. He wrote "God Bless America" to express his thanks to the United States for the opportunities it had provided. George and Ira Gershwin, who wrote musical comedies, were the sons of Russian immigrants. The popular Marx Brothers grew up on the Lower East Side. Other famous Jewish comedians included Jack Benny and Milton Berle.

Several eastern European Jews dominated the U.S. movie industry in its early years. Louis B. Mayer, Samuel Goldwyn,

Adolph Zukor, Harry Cohn, and the Warner Brothers created and ran Hollywood's motion picture studios.

Rising Anti-Semitism

Anti-Semitism in the United States had grown during the 1920s, and it continued to rise during the next decade. Part of this was due to social and economic tensions caused by the Great Depression, which gripped the nation during the 1930s. Anti-Semitic groups arose, and there were incidents of violence against Jews.

Millions of Americans listened to the anti-Semitic radio broadcasts of Father Charles Coughlin, who blamed Jewish bankers for the Depression. Another factor in growing anti-Semitism was the war brewing in Europe. Isolationists wanted to keep the United States out of European affairs, and some accused Jews of trying to get the United States involved.

▲ The tradition of Yiddish entertainment was a vital part of Jewish American life. This poster from the late 1930s advertises a musical comedy presented by the Works Project Administration (WPA), a federal program to create work during the Great Depression.

The Holocaust

As the Jewish American community was growing in the United States, Jews living in Europe were being massacred. The Holocaust is the worst episode of anti-Semitic persecution in history. Between 1933, when Adolf Hitler and his Nazi Party rose to power in Germany, and 1945, when Germany was defeated in World War II, 6 million Jews were murdered, including 1.5 million children. The Holocaust wiped out two-thirds of all the Jews in Europe.

Hitler hated the Jews. When he came to power in Germany, he passed laws taking away German Jews' rights and encouraged

Germans to attack Jews. He also began sending Jews to camps where they were used as slave labor. The Jews worked from dawn to dusk, with little food or water and the constant threat of physical punishment. Thousands died under these brutal conditions.

Germany invaded Poland in 1939, starting World War II. In 1941, the Nazis decided on a "final solution" to what they called the "Jewish problem": completely get rid of all the Jews in Europe. New concentration camps, or death camps, were built just for killing Jews. The most deaths were in Poland, where 90 percent of the Jewish population (about three million people) was killed.

The American Response to Nazism

Even before the world awoke to the full horrors of the Holocaust, Jewish Americans tried to take steps against Hitler. In the 1930s, Jewish groups organized a nationwide boycott of German goods. Jewish organizations also

"In 1944 we were all taken—my parents, my family— to concentration camps. I lost my parents, a sister and a brother. . . . Bergen-Belsen . . . was one of the worst camps. People were dying of disease and hunger everywhere. You just stepped over dead people."

Tilly Stimler, who entered a concentration camp as a teenager and moved to the United States after World War II

▼ A huge crowd filled Madison Square Garden in New York City in 1937 as Jewish Americans and other protesters came to protest against Nazi atrocities in Europe.

staged rallies at Madison Square Garden in New York City in 1933 and again in 1937. They drew thousands of anti-Nazi protesters. Despite these efforts, however, neither President Franklin D. Roosevelt nor the U.S. Congress took steps to halt the Holocaust.

By the late 1930s, it became clear that German Jews desperately needed to escape from Europe and Nazi persecution. Jewish American leaders begged Roosevelt and Congress to lift U.S. immigration limits, allowing more Jews into the country. They refused. The United States eventually entered World War II in December 1941 and helped defeat Hitler. Although the victory ended Nazism, it did almost nothing to save the Jews of Europe.

Opening the Door

Some Jews had been able to leave Germany in the early days of Hitler's reign. Among them was Albert Einstein, the most famous scientist of all time. Other Jews emigrated after World War II. Between 1948 and 1950, the Displaced Persons Act permitted about two hundred thousand Europeans (Jews and non-Jews) to enter the United States. This number represented only a fraction of the total number of 1.5 million to 2 million people who had been displaced by the war (20 percent of whom were Jewish). Thousands of European Jews, however, did take advantage of this opening and found refuge in the United States. Among them was the writer Elie Wiesel, a concentration camp survivor from Hungary. Wiesel is best known for his

▲ Albert Einstein (*left*) was working in the United States when Hitler came to power. He did not return to Germany but stayed in the United States, where he is shown receiving his citizenship papers in 1940.

> "Let us remember, let us remember the heroes of Warsaw, the martyrs of Treblinka, the children of Auschwitz. They fought alone, they suffered alone, they lived alone, but they did not die alone, for something in all of us died with them."
>
> *Elie Wiesel, report of the President's Commission on the Holocaust, 1979*

▲ Elie Wiesel, Jewish American author and survivor of the Holocaust, speaks at a pro-Israel rally in Washington, D.C., in 2002. The United States has been a strong supporter of Israel since the Jewish nation was founded in 1948.

book *Night*, which tells the story of his experience in the camps. Wiesel won the Nobel Peace Prize in 1986 and has dedicated his life to making sure that no one forgets the Holocaust.

Zionism and the Nation of Israel

The horrors of the Holocaust and the sad situation of all the displaced people made many Jews want a homeland in the Middle East, in the region called Palestine. Their movement was called Zionism. Zionists faced many hurdles. Britain was governing Palestine, where both Jews and Arabs lived. There was fighting between the two groups, and Britain would only admit very few Jews to the region, both during and after World War II.

Soon after the end of the war, Zionist organizations in the United States launched an all-out campaign. They put pressure on the United States and the United Nations to help establish a Jewish homeland. Jewish American leaders appealed to President Harry S. Truman for help. On November 29, 1947, the United Nations divided Palestine into three parts: a Jewish state, an Arab state, and an international zone around Jerusalem. On May 14, 1948, the new State of Israel proclaimed its independence.

After the Holocaust, many Jewish Americans realized anew the importance of their Jewish identity. They supported Israel and joined synagogues or Jewish organizations, both religious and non-religious. Building a strong Jewish community in the United States and abroad had become a high priority.

The Arrival of Soviet Jews

Soviet and Russian Jews make up the most recent wave of Jewish immigration. Until the mid-1970s, the Soviet Union strictly limited the number of Jews who were allowed to leave the country. Jews had long been persecuted there and were not allowed to practice their religion. Many wanted to emigrate. Starting in 1975, the Soviet government began to loosen its immigration restrictions. Between 1975 and 1987, about 110,000 Soviet Jews immigrated to the United States. Many of them settled in New York City, while others spread out through the Northeast and Midwest.

In 1991, the Soviet Union officially broke up into different countries. Russia, the largest, allowed more Jews to leave. Between the late 1970s and the year 2000, some four hundred thousand Jews from either the Soviet Union or former Soviet countries immigrated to the United States. Mainly because they could not practice their religion in their homelands, these Jews are somewhat less religious than other Jews in the United States. They are also somewhat poorer than other Jewish Americans, in part because many cannot find the same types of jobs or practice the professions they had at home. Like the Jewish immigrants who came before them, however, Soviet Jews are both adapting to and transforming the Jewish American cultural landscape.

"Just by the fluke of where I was born, I had been safe while others perished. I used to stand in front of the mirror, look myself in the eye, and say, 'You're a Jew, and if you had been there, you would be dead.'"

Phyllis Taylor, a Jewish American from New York City, on how she was haunted by the Holocaust

▸ Among the Soviet Jews who immigrated to the United States was Yuri Balovlenkov (*right*), shown arriving in 1987. His wife and daughters had waited since 1979 for him to get permission to leave the Soviet Union.

Jewish Americans in U.S. Society

Today, according to the American Jewish Committee, 5.3 million Jews live in the United States. (Some sources say there are more, depending on how strictly one defines being Jewish.) The current figure is slightly less than the 5.5 million predicted in 1990. It is now believed that the Jewish American population will continue to decrease slowly because of a low birthrate among Jewish women. Although the U.S. is home to more Jews than anywhere else in the world, trends indicate that Israel may soon move into first place.

Many Jews are concerned about the shrinking population as they try to maintain their religion and cultural identity. Intermarriage rates have increased slightly in the last twenty years—today, close to half of all Jews marry non-Jews. Only about one-third of the children born to intermarried Jews are being raised as Jews.

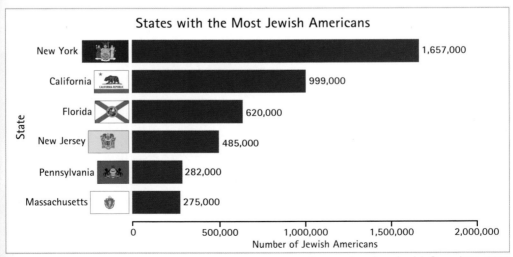

States with the Most Jewish Americans

State	Number of Jewish Americans
New York	1,657,000
California	999,000
Florida	620,000
New Jersey	485,000
Pennsylvania	282,000
Massachusetts	275,000

Source: American Jewish Committee, 2000

▲ This chart shows the states where the greatest numbers of Jewish Americans live. Reflecting early settlement patterns, New York also has the highest percentage (8.7 percent) of Jewish Americans, followed by New Jersey (5.8 percent).

Jews live in all parts of the country. According to the National Jewish Population Survey (NJPS), conducted in 2000–2001, more Jews—43 percent—live in the Northeast than in any other region. Only 13 percent of Jews make their homes in the Midwest, the region with the fewest Jews.

Education and Work

On the whole, Jewish Americans are better educated, have higher-status jobs, and make more money than the rest of the U.S. population. According to the NJPS, more than half of Jewish Americans (55 percent) have graduated college and earned a bachelor's degree. This is compared to only 28 percent of non-Jews. A quarter of Jewish American adults have earned a graduate degree, compared to only 5 percent of non-Jews.

The median household income of Jewish Americans is about $50,000; for all U.S. households, the median income is $42,000. Most Jewish workers (61 percent) have high-status jobs in professional or technical fields such as health care, business, finance, politics, and law. In the past, the most distinguished professionals included doctors Jonas Salk and Albert Sabin, who discovered important vaccines. Louis Brandeis, who became the first Jew on the U.S. Supreme Court in 1916, was one of the most respected judges in U.S. history. Today, two Jewish Americans, Ruth Bader Ginsburg and Stephen Breyer, sit on the Supreme Court. In 2000, the Democratic Party nominated a Jew, Senator Joseph Lieberman, as its vice presidential candidate.

◀ U.S. Supreme Court Justice Ruth Bader Ginsburg, photographed in 2005, is of German Jewish descent. She was appointed to the Supreme Court in 1993.

A Wide Range of Organizations

Despite the inroads Jews have made economically and socially, many struggle to get by. Today, 5 percent of Jewish household incomes fall below the U.S. poverty line. Poverty is more common among single mothers, the elderly, and those with a high school education or less. Numerous Jewish social service organizations provide a range of services to needy Jewish Americans.

Tzedaka—giving charity and doing righteous acts—is one of the most important Jewish commandments, and as a whole, Jews have always been generous. There are many Jewish charitable, civic, religious, and political organizations. The American Jewish Committee is one of the most important. It began in 1906 after pogroms swept through eastern Europe. Today, it sponsors conferences promoting Jewish identity and human rights for Jews worldwide. The Hebrew Immigrant Aid Society, founded in the early 1900s, still provides services to both Jewish and non-Jewish immigrants and refugees.

The largest Jewish organization in the United States is Hadassah, a women's group originally created to help Jews and Arabs in Palestine. Another organization, the Anti-Defamation League, is the world's most important group fighting anti-Semitism.

Protecting Historical Memory

Many Jews work to make sure no one forgets the Holocaust. They have helped raise funds for the United States Holocaust Memorial Museum in Washington, D.C., which opened in 1993, and gathered

▼ Visitors to the United States Holocaust Memorial Museum pass under a metal sign copied from one hanging over the entrance to the Auschwitz death camp. The German phrase *Arbeit Macht Frei* translates as "Work makes one free."

▲ Movie director and founder of the Shoah Foundation Steven Spielberg (*left*) gives direction on the set of the 1993 movie *Schindler's List*. The movie tells the story of the efforts of one man—a non-Jewish German—to save Jews during the Holocaust.

the memories and oral histories of Holocaust survivors. They also work to ensure that the history of the Holocaust is taught in schools.

In 1994, film director Steven Spielberg founded the Shoah Foundation. It saves the testimony of Holocaust survivors to make sure their stories are not lost. In partnership with the Anti-Defamation League and the Israeli group Yad Vashem, the Shoah Foundation has developed a high school curriculum called "Echoes and Reflections." Through the study of the Holocaust, students learn to confront racism and discrimination in daily life.

"It has always been my dream that the Shoah Foundation's unique archive of testimonies would transform the way history is taught and learned. . . . Today, that dream is becoming a reality. The partnership . . . ensures that future generations can learn what survivors and other eyewitnesses to the Holocaust can teach: that our very humanity depends on the practice of tolerance and mutual respect."

Steven Spielberg, on the Shoah Foundation's Holocaust curriculum

Cultural Contributions

Jewish Americans have made many cultural contributions to the United States. The works of playwrights Arthur Miller and Neil Simon have enriched U.S. theater. Major American writers include Norman Mailer, Philip Roth, and Saul Bellow. We listen to the music of composers Richard Rodgers, Oscar Hammerstein II, Leonard Bernstein, and Stephen Sondheim. Many current entertainers—such as violinist Itzhak Perlman, actor/directors Woody Allen and Mel Brooks, comedian Jerry Seinfeld, and singers Beverly Sills and Barbra Streisand—are continuing the rich traditions of Jewish stars of the past, such as Al Jolson, George Burns, and Danny Kaye.

Being Jewish

Most Jewish Americans see being Jewish as very important, and they connect with the Jewish community in some way. Fewer than half of all Jewish Americans belong to a synagogue, but a larger number observe the High Holidays—Rosh Hashanah (the Jewish New Year) and Yom Kippur, the Day of Atonement. Jewish Americans also often celebrate the eight-day holiday of Passover by gathering for a special meal called a *seder*. Passover commemorates the Jews' exodus from Egypt thousands of years ago, when they won freedom from slavery. The seder reminds Jews—especially children—of the struggles of their ancestors for freedom.

Other ways of staying connected include taking classes at Jewish community centers and sending children to Jewish schools, including Sunday schools. In the 1960s, "prayer fellowships" began. These small groups—called *havurot*—meet informally, often in people's homes, to pray, study, talk, laugh, and sometimes argue

◀ Orthodox Jews in Brooklyn, New York, celebrate the beginning of Passover with the traditional burning of bread. Orthodox Jewish Americans are very strict in their religious observances.

about what it means to be Jewish. In such settings, thousands of Jewish Americans are developing more deeply rooted Jewish identities.

Non-religious Jews still identify themselves as Jewish. They may support Israel and identify with Jewish culture—food, customs, music, and comedy. They deal with the tensions that sometimes come with being a member of a minority in a Christian-dominated culture—having to explain, for example, that they celebrate Hanukkah when most Americans celebrate Christmas.

It may be inside the home that the Jewish American spirit most freely appears. Many Jewish Americans say they feel the strongest sense of community when they share a meal with family and friends. The community of Jewish Americans may be too diverse for anyone to predict exactly where it's headed. It is likely, however, that the deep desire for community that has sustained Jewish American culture for more than 350 years will continue to do so.

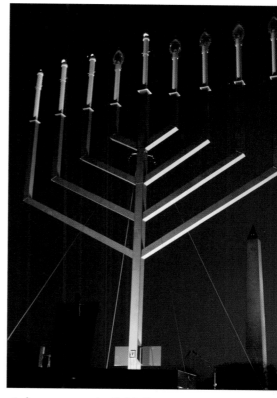

▲ A ceremony to light the National Hanukkah Menorah takes place every year in Washington, D.C. The giant menorah symbolizes the place of Jewish Americans in U.S. society.

Yiddish Lives On

For hundreds of years, Yiddish was the language of eastern European Jews. A rich and colorful language, it blends early German, Hebrew, Polish, Russian, and other languages. At one time, people thought Yiddish was dying, but it lives on. Many universities now offer courses in Yiddish studies. The YIVO Institute for Jewish Research has been studying the Yiddish language and culture of Ashkenazic Jews since 1923, and the National Yiddish Book Center has collected more than 1.5 million Yiddish books since 1980. Today, many Yiddish words are used in regular conversation. Here are some of them: *bagel* (a hard donut-shaped roll), *chutzpah* (a lot of nerve), *kvetch* (someone who complains, or to complain), *lox* (smoked salmon, often eaten with bagels), *mensch* (a good person), and *schlep* (to carry or drag around).

Notable Jewish Americans

Bella Abzug (1920–1998) U.S.-born daughter of Russian Jewish parents who served three terms in the U.S. Congress as a Democrat from New York (1971–1977). She fought for women's rights, social and economic justice, and antiwar efforts.

Leonard Bernstein (1918–1990) U.S.-born son of Russian Jewish parents who earned worldwide acclaim as a composer and conductor of both classical and popular music.

Albert Einstein (1879–1955) Brilliant German physicist and Nobel Prize winner who came to the United States to work at Princeton University and became a U.S. citizen in 1940. His theory of relativity made him the most famous scientist of all time.

Ruth Bader Ginsburg (1933–) Associate justice of the U.S. Supreme Court since 1993, born in Brooklyn, New York, who is considered a staunch defender of constitutional rights to privacy and equality for women.

Albert A. Michelson (1852–1931) Prussian-born physicist who came to the United States as a young child and became known for determining methods for measuring the speed of light. In 1907, he became the first American to win a Nobel Prize for science.

Adolph S. Ochs (1858–1935) Newspaper publisher, the son of German Jewish immigrants, who in 1896 acquired control of the *New York Times* and built it into one of the world's most influential newspapers.

Jonas Salk (1914–1995) Medical researcher, born in New York to Russian Jewish immigrants, who developed the vaccine that wiped out polio, a disease that had crippled and paralyzed thousands of Americans—most of them children—every year.

Isaac Bashevis Singer (1904–1991) Novelist and short-story writer who could speak only three words of English when he arrived in the United States from Poland in 1935 and went on to win numerous literary awards for his works in Yiddish, including the Nobel Prize for Literature in 1978.

Isaac Stern (1920–2001) Gifted violinist who emigrated from Russia to San Francisco in 1921, became a soloist with the San Francisco Symphony by age eleven, and played concerts throughout the world.

Kerri Strug (1977–) U.S.-born gymnast who won a team bronze medal in the 1992 Olympic Games at age fourteen and went on to win a team gold medal in the 1996 Olympic Games.

Time Line

1095   The Crusades begin; thousands of Jews and Muslims are killed over the next few hundred years.

1492   The Jews of Spain are expelled during the Inquisition.

1654   Twenty-three Sephardic Jews from Recife, Brazil, arrive in New Amsterdam and form the first Jewish community in North America.

1763   Touro Synagogue in Newport, Rhode Island, is consecrated.

1819   Rebecca Gratz founds the Female Hebrew Benevolent Society.

1820   Large numbers of German Jews begin to immigrate to the United States.

1843   Twelve German Jewish immigrants in New York form B'nai B'rith.

1873   Union of American Hebrew Congregations is founded.

1875   Hebrew Union College, a school for Reform rabbis, is founded.

1881   Violent pogroms begin in eastern Europe, spurring the Great Migration.

1893   Hannah Solomon founds the National Council of Jewish Women in Chicago.

1903   Pogrom in Kishinev in eastern Europe kills fifty Jews and leaves five hundred wounded.

1906   American Jewish Committee is founded.

1911   March 25: A fire at the Triangle Shirtwaist Factory in New York kills 146 workers, mostly Jewish and Italian immigrant women.

1916   Louis Brandeis becomes the first Jew appointed to the U.S. Supreme Court.

1921   Congress passes a law limiting immigration and putting quotas on the number of immigrants from each nation.

1924   National Origins Act further limits immigration, ending the great wave of eastern European Jewish immigration.

1933   Adolf Hitler begins his rise to power in Germany, leading to the persecution of European Jews and eventually to the Holocaust, during which six million Jews are killed.

1948   May 14: The nation of Israel is proclaimed.

1948–1950   Displaced Persons Act permits the entry of about two hundred thousand Europeans into the United States.

1975   Soviet Jews are allowed to emigrate; by 1987, about 110,000 enter the United States.

1993   United States Holocaust Memorial Museum opens in Washington, D.C.

1994   Steven Spielberg founds the Shoah Foundation to preserve the testimony of Holocaust survivors.

2000   Senator Joseph Lieberman becomes the first Jew nominated by a major U.S. political party as its vice presidential candidate.

Glossary

anti-Semitism prejudice against Jews

Ashkenazim Jews of central or eastern European origin

Bar Mitzvah attainment by Jewish boys of the age of religious duty

boycott refusal to do business with certain companies or nations to protest their policies

culture language, beliefs, customs, and ways of life shared by a group of people from the same region or nation

dry goods merchandise such as fabrics, thread, needles, and buttons

emigrate leave one nation or region to go and live in another place

exile state of being forced or feeling compelled to leave a homeland

ghetto neighborhood of a city, usually poor, where people of the same race, religion, or ethnic group live

heritage something handed down from previous generations

Holocaust systematic murder of six million Jews by Nazi Germany and its allies during World War II

immigrant person who arrives in a new nation or region to take up residence

intellectual person who spends a lot of time studying and thinking

isolationist person who does not want his or her nation involved in the political and economic affairs of other nations

kosher following Jewish dietary laws under which certain foods (such as pork and shellfish) are unacceptable, while other, acceptable foods must be prepared in a special way

labor union organization, often in a particular trade or business, that represents the rights of workers

Muslim having to do with (or a follower of) the religion of Islam

peasant person of low social status who generally worked on farms

pogrom riot directed against a specific group of people, with the intention of hurting or killing them and burning and looting their property

prejudice bias against or dislike of a person or group because of race, nationality, or other factors

quota assigned proportion; in the case of immigration, a limit on the number of immigrants allowed from a particular country

rabbi Jewish religious leader and teacher

refugee person who leaves a country or region because of conflict, natural disaster, or persecution

Sephardic having to do with Jews of Spanish or Portuguese origin

socialism economic system, based on cooperation rather than competition, under which members of society collectively own and control the production of some goods and services

steerage section of a steamship that provided poor accommodation and was used by passengers who could not afford cabins

synagogue Jewish house of worship

tenement poorly built and crowded apartment building with bad ventilation and sanitation and low safety standards

Further Resources

Books

Downing, David. *Persecution and Emigration.* World Almanac® Library of the Holocaust (series). World Almanac® Library, 2006.

Finkelstein, Norman H. *Forged in Freedom: Shaping the Jewish-American Experience.* Jewish Publication Society of America, 2002.

Haberle, Susan E. *Jewish Immigrants 1880–1924.* Coming to America (series). Blue Earth Books, 2003.

Rubin, Susan Goldman. *L'Chaim! To Jewish Life in America! Celebrating from 1654 until Today.* Harry N. Abrams, 2004.

Web Sites

From Haven to Home: 350 Years of Jewish Life in America
www.loc.gov/exhibits/haventohome
Online exhibit on Jews in America from 1654 to 2004

The Jewish Virtual Library
www.jewishvirtuallibrary.org/jsource
Online encyclopedia covering Jews in America and other Jewish topics

The Statue of Liberty–Ellis Island Foundation
www.ellisisland.org/genealogy/ellis_island.asp
Records of Ellis Island arrivals, stories of immigrant families, and immigration time line

Publisher's note to educators and parents: Our editors have carefully reviewed these Web sites to ensure that they are suitable for children. Many Web sites change frequently, however, and we cannot guarantee that a site's future contents will continue to meet our high standards of quality and educational value. Be advised that children should be closely supervised whenever they access the Internet.

Where to Visit

Lower East Side Tenement Museum
108 Orchard Street
New York, NY 10002
Telephone: (212) 982-8420
www.tenement.org

About the Author

Amy Stone has written several books for children, ranging from biographies of famous women to histories of the Creek and Oneida Indians. She lives in Milwaukee, Wisconsin.

Index